QWAVA

QWAVA tells the story of the Murmedons, survivors of destroyed planets turned resistance fighters who pursue the Aryas throughout the universe to prevent the plunder and destruction of water-rich planets. One by one the Murmedons grow in number as the Aryas annihilate all that stands in their way of harvesting the universe's most sacred resource: water. With high-octane action, adventure, and memorable characters, QWAVA is a series of interconnected tales that are sure to engage, inspire, and entertain. This then, is the story of how Kai Onakea was saved from the desert planet once known as Earth.

978-1-927028-14-8

QWAVA

Colin Michaels

QWAVA

Book 1

Without water we were destined to perish. We had been too distracted with war to realize what we were losing, and what we were losing was the most sacred resource in the universe, the one resource that made life possible. There were countless names for it. We called it water, the Ancients called it qwava. The corrupt leaders of the planet who had colluded with the Ancients had been deceived. Even they had been left behind to face the survivors of the planet. They were all tortured and executed for their crimes against the planet, for their treason. The cities crumbled into chaos, the oceans turned to deserts, men became beasts and began to feed off other men. Men unified to survive, then divided to survive. Eventually what little qwava the Ancients had left behind began to run out and life began to dwindle, to shrivel up and disappear--species by species, being by being, cell by cell. When at last the Murmedons entered the planet's orbit searching for remnants of life, it was already too late. Earth had become yet another lifeless desert planet. Hoping to salvage and study the life that had once existed on the planet, the Murmedons released their hovering life probes, and collected DNA samples for safe storage. And just when they were about to leave the planet, they spotted a small blinking life form on their sensors staggering across the great endless desert that had once been the Pacific Ocean. A survivor. The last of the planet.

QWAVA

It had taken days for Jake Onakea to find water. He and his twelve-year-old son Kai had come across yet another destroyed scavenger camp in the Pacific Desert, a desert they were trying to negotiate in their search for a refuge called 'Eden'. Or at least that's what Jake had called it. That wasn't an official name. That was his name for it inspired by the few post-apocalyptic films and he had seen, and to Kai he had described it as a scientific community that had been formed before the Great Calamity in order to preserve humanity. Jake had described farms and orchards wherever the eye looked and more than enough water for everyone. Enough water so that no one had to kill each other for it. Enough water so that they could drink at least one glass of water every day and bathe every second day. He had described it so many times that he was actually beginning to believe this place he called 'Eden' actually existed. He was actually starting to believe his own story. Truth was he wasn't sure if it did exist or if it didn't. He had heard talks about such a place during the great water wars and rebellions. He had heard talk of camps and water containers and engineered farms

QWAVA

that could produce enough daily food to sustain a small city. Scientists had been preparing for the worst just in case they lost all the oceans, seas and rivers. And they had, and he had never heard about the secret communities again. But he remembered the movies. The clichés. The Eden communities amidst a world filled with zombies. There were no zombies. What there was…was a lot worse. People tearing each other apart for the last drop of water. Scavengers. Now Jake continued telling the story of Eden over and over again, telling how everything would be fine once they reached Eden, trying to convince himself as much as he tried to convince his son. It was the one thing, the only thing, that gave his son hope, and he wouldn't take that away from him, especially since every other camp they happened upon were scenes of indescribable carnage and horror. This camp they scavenged now was no exception.

It was no surprise. Everyone had turned against each other for water, and everyone had perished before anyone could enjoy what water was left in the few containers that had been hidden around

QWAVA

the camp. There was no survivor. There was no vic-
tor. There usually never was. The desert made sure
of this.

When Jake had first encountered these
camps and these scenes of carnage, he had tried to
shelter Kai; he had tried to keep his son's eyes away
from the truth of what was happening to humanity.
But the camps and the scenes became more and
more frequent as the days grew hotter and hotter
and the water grew scarcer and scarcer; soon Jake
realized his son needed to see the truth for himself,
needed to understand what was happening so that
he would take his self-defense courses his father
tried to teach him a little more seriously. One day he
would need to use them and he needed to be fear-
less or else he would end up like one of the boys or
girls they had found in the camps.

Together Jake and Kai had scavenged
dozens of camps since the Ancients had robbed their
planet of its water, and always Jake told his son
about how they had fooled everyone. They had
seemingly come from nowhere, and yet they had
somehow been with humanity for centuries, hiding in

QWAVA

the shadows, bribing the rich with promises of limitless power as they slowly change the planet's atmosphere and waited for the right time to begin the final stages of what had been called the 'Blue Harvest' by independent news sources-news sources that weren't under control of the rich and powerful and who could still report the truth. What was happening to the government and news, the corporate takeover of government and news, should have been the first sign. And it was, only no one was paying attention.

The Ancients were humanoids, and looked like albinos with white skin, blue eyes, and white hair like snow. When they were first discovered accidentally, the mainstream media, controlled by the rich and powerful, called them the Ancients and portrayed them as friendly grandparents who were simply here to help humanity evolve to another level of spiritual consciousness like Columbus in the New World. The media called them the Ancients, but they called themselves the Aryas, and the Aryas were centuries ahead of humans in technology, and had such a strong ability to focus and use their minds

QWAVA

that they could learn any language in a few hours and speak like a native of almost any planet. Their original language wasn't strange or unnatural to the ears. Their language actually sounded very much like the Latin of Rome, and, indeed they had been here since then conducting surveys on the planet. The Ancients had prepared the world like a chess game. They had divided it, distracted it, destroyed it; they had made sure that when they were ready to harvest they wouldn't waste any costly resources fighting natives especially since they were outnumbered forty to one. The Ancients had the technology but not the numbers nor the willpower of a native defending their home; so they needed to be clever, and they had learned this truth the hard way.
In the beginning the Ancients used direct tyranny to divide and control planets, taking control of kings and kingdoms, introducing a class system in one area, a caste system in another. When kingdoms and empires were toppled, because they could be, because everyone knew who was responsible for the oppression, abuse and tyranny, they changed their tactics so that everything would be invisible, if not

QWAVA

invisible vague, so that no one would know who to blame, revolt against or topple to end tyranny. They changed their king-structure to an economic one, to corporate-structure, a structure that would usher in the industrial revolution and would initiate the slow process of warming the atmosphere to prepare the planet's temperature to maximize qwava extraction. The natives were upset, were angry, were ready to revolt as the planet warmed and the atmosphere thickened with industry, but this time there was no regime to revolt against, no one king to bring down, just a few corporations who controlled many kings and many regimes. Faceless monsters that had many heads. Just as soon as natives severed one, three or four other heads grew in its stead.
In less than a century, corporations replaced tsars, emperors and kings, and the Ancients could prepare the board for the end game without fear of ever being toppled like a king. One corporation could control several kings, several governments, and rebelling and toppling a corporation, whose tyranny thrived on immeasurable borderless greed, whose actions were sneaky and surreptitious and hidden

and protected by laws and paperwork and presidents and politicians and world trade organizers who owed their power and positions to them, was a difficult if not an impossible affair. The corporations were the new kings, kings of the world, and they worked hard, very hard, day and night, to realize the Ancient mandate. Pollute to plunder. Divide to conquer. Preach to hide. This was back then and remains today the Ancient modus operandi. At one time many believed the British originated the 'divide and rule' strategy. Divide and rule wasn't a British strategy. It had never been. It had always been an Ancient strategy. The Ancients had taught the British this strategy as they led one of their first corporations, the East India Company into the world to do their polluting, plundering, killing and dividing. The East India Company was their test case on Earth, and they soon found that as a corporation in control of several kings they could get away with concentration camps in Africa, slaughter in India, incalculable genocide in North America--unthinkable crimes against humanity for which the British Crown nor the British Raj could not really be held responsible. No one was held respon-

QWAVA

sible except for the corporation, and the corporation had too many heads to be executed for its crimes. As the ice melted and the time for the blue harvest came closer and closer, the Ancients, as though they were fertilizing a crop, introduced new technology in small doses, century by century, country by country, depending on which country was in power. First the French. Then the British. Then the Germans. Then the Americans. And finally the Chinese. And when humanity had been given just enough technology to destroy themselves, but not enough to threaten the Ancients, the wars began and every nation shocked and awed each other to bits and pieces for crude oil and living space without once considering what was really at stake.

It had taken a hundred years for most of the ice to melt and flood the world. A hundred years to drown entire countries and wipe out entire populations. And it had taken the Ancients less than twenty to empty the planet. To drain the oceans and turn a water -rich planet into a desert planet. By then humanity was so divided and full of fear and hatred that no one realized what was happening. They

QWAVA

couldn't even see what the real enemy was doing to their planet. They just observed the great big space cruisers in the sky and the lowering water levels with each passing day distracted by winning a war that could not be won. Instead of trying to stop the Ancients they asked for better weapons to kill their enemies, and better weapons they received. When the Ancients had finished and the great oceans were empty, Earth was nothing more than a withering ball of heat and dust and there was nothing left but the all-pervading scent of death and corruption and pockets of defeated humanity scrambling for food and water. And as the last of humanity fought for drops of water, the Ancients returned to their planet where they sold their qwava at a premium and engaged in debates on the morality of stealing sacred resources from interplanetary natives who they described as savages and possessed all the media they needed to support their accusations. War. Genocide. Cannibalism. Media that appalled most of the Aryas population, and it was really only a minority of the Aryas population that challenged what was being presented as truth and accused the

QWAVA

qwava fairing corporations of presenting only one side of the story.

The camp was small. Seven canvas tents flapping in the dusk wind, and within each tent there were all kinds of relics from the old world: a bag of bottle caps, dusty old dolls, rusted knives and busted rifles, silverware, a bag of diamonds and other jewels that had been used as chips for heated games of poker. There was also a solar powered dune-buggy hooked up to a massive caravan in which these scavengers seemed to travel the Pacific Desert. Jake inspected the buggy. He pushed the red button to start the engine. Nothing happened. He pushed it again. Again, nothing. He had suspected as much. The dust had gotten into the panels and engine and had rendered it inoperable. Now there wasn't much that could be done. He would have liked to have stayed in the camp and tried to fix it, but it was too danger-ous to stay put in any one place for too long, and they needed to fill their flasks with whatever water remained in the metal rain tanks and find another camp; or, if they were lucky, Eden.

QWAVA

Jake gave the buggy one long angry look, and then kicked it in frustration. He figured it must have broken down and panic must have slowly settled in on the camp as everyone realized they would be on foot under the sweltering, unforgiving sun. It was clear. No one had attacked these scavengers. These scavengers had turned against themselves. There were also hints of cannibalism, which was not uncommon among the scavengers. Remnants of thigh bones and collar bones and toes and fingers in the communal cooking fire. He had also found some heavily spiced meat in little tin containers which was still edible; but after much sniffing and imagining he couldn't quite figure out what kind of meat it was, and he wasn't taking any chances, especially not with Kai. They hadn't resorted to cannibalism yet, and he had promised himself and his late wife that they never would. Now there was only the water, the broken-down buggy and the bodies. The scavengers had killed each other for food and water and he and Kai had buried the bodies and said a prayer for their souls.

Kicking the dusty yellow buggy in frustra-

QWAVA

tion, Jake turned to face Kai who was still rummaging through the canvas tents searching for food. "Find anything?" he asked. His son wore a rich khaki jumper his mother had made for him, sunglasses to protect him from the sweltering sun, and a red bandana to protect his young face from the hard sandstorms. He carried a long sheathed knife for protection, but had never had to use it. In his inner pocket he had a picture of his mother and father before the invasion and the harvest. Both of them in the calm ocean with their chins on a surfboard staring at him when he was about three-years-old.

Kai turned to his father and held up a can of peas. "Can of peas," he said. It had been hidden under a pillow, buried deep in the ground. He had noticed the earth had been disturbed under the pillow and he had seen this many times before. It didn't seem like a good place to hide a can since everyone thought of it. Yet without fail most scavengers dug holes in their tents to bury and hide their salvage.

"That's good. There's water in those cans. We'll keep it for later. Keep searching."

Kai nodded and continued searching the

QWAVA

tents to see if anyone had buried any more canned goods. In one tent, under a sleeping bag he spotted something that flashed in a stream of blinding white sunlight, something he had never seen before. It was the size of a book, thinner, with a shiny metal casing and solar panels. "Dad!" he called from inside the shadowy tent. "Come! Come quick!"

Jake came rushing in. "What is it?"

"That's what I wanna know?" Kai handed him the small metal case.

Jake looked it over a moment. "It's a computer" he said. "It's been tampered with so that it can charge in the sun like the buggy." He stared at the side and it had a key port, and he wondered if it could read the storage key he had in his rucksack with all his videos and pictures and songs and all kinds of personal memories of the old world. Maybe it could, and maybe he could finally show them to Kai, and show him what it was like when the world teemed with water and life. Or maybe he wouldn't. Maybe seeing what it was like before would only make the desert more unbearable than it already was. Maybe not remembering was better. Better for

QWAVA

Kai at least.

"Can you turn it on?"

Jake tried, then he shook his head. He scrutinized the computer for a moment and soon realized it was out of power. "It needs to be charged," he said. "Shouldn't take long. This is Ancient tech."

"Even the computer."

"Not by the looks of it. Just the solar paneling."

Kai knew most of Ancient technology harnessed star energy in ways humanity had never even fathomed. At one time engineers had tinkered with solar technology, but the Ancients had purposefully led humanity toward a primitive, scarce form of energy that had served three purposes: launch humanity into war over a useless resource; prepare the atmosphere for their blue harvest; and forever limit humanity to their planet. They wanted to ground humanity. Make sure they never had the means for interstellar travel which required limitless and abundant energy that could come from two main sources: dark matter or star energy. The Ancients had the ability to harness both like a sail harnessing wind for their interstellar conquests.

"What do you think's on it?"

His dad shook his head. "Don't know. I'll leave it to charge and we can check tomorrow." He patted his boy on the head. "Good find."
Kai smiled, and Jake saw his mother in his smile and went inward for a moment. Then he took the computer, quit the tent, and laid it out in the sun. He hadn't seen a computer for a long time. Since the desertification of their world, it was like technology hadn't even existed except for a reminder here and there like this one.

Later that evening they sat by a small fire sharing a small glass of water.

"Tell about how it was," Kai asked. He asked this every night, and every night Jake told him a small story of how it was before the Ancients had destroyed their world.

"Well," Jake answered, "when I was growing up there was water right where we're sitting. Not just a little. Tons. There was water everywhere.
There was water everywhere and the surfing was

QWAVA

never better. Everywhere you looked there was water. Clear, blue water. So beautiful and blue it hurt your eyes. And you, well you came out with me every morning as a little boy, but I don't think you remember that. I used to float you on the board and you used to get so calm on that board. In fact anytime you'd cry, the only way to get you to stop was to get you on a board and in the water."

He shook his head and smiled at the memory. Then he looked to his son and watched the firelight dance over his face. He continued: "I'd place you on the board and we'd paddle out and we'd watch the sun climb up the horizon. I'd want to catch a wave with you, but your mom would scream that you were too young and that floating on the board was enough. So we'd float there on the board and just watch the dawn with the other surfers who had come out to do the same. You would get so calm on the board. It was like the deep blue of the ocean was the only thing that would calm you."

Jake lost himself in the memory, and after a moment he mumbled: "We had everything then and we didn't even know it…that's why they were able to steal it from us." Then he vented a sigh of despair and went silent for a long moment as Kai watched the bitter past come alive in his watery eyes. Suddenly, in the darkness of the desert, a flash of light flickered and signaled. Another flash responded. Scavengers were closing in on them. With a start, Jake held his son's arm. He would have put out the fire but he realized it was already too late. Then Kai spotted them, saw their silhouettes in the moonlight.

"Dad," Kai said. He had seen the signal as well.

"I know, Kai," his father answered calmly. "I need you to be calm and I need you to listen to me." Kai nodded. "Quickly fill the flasks. Can you do that for me? Can you fill them up?" Kai nodded again and didn't waste another second. He grabbed the empty flasks and filled them at the tanks and tried not to think of the scavengers approaching them in the darkness like a pack of wolves. Jake grabbed their belongings and packed the computer safely in a rucksack.

Within minutes Kai returned with seven flasks filled with water. "We just gonna leave the

QWAVA

rest?" Kai asked with concern in his voice. Jake nodded. "Yeah, we're just gonna leave it." Kai didn't seem to understand. But his father added: "It's no good to us dead."

Kai said nothing more about the water, but suddenly heard something clang in the shadows. "Did you hear?" He asked his father in a small, choked voice.

"I heard," Jake answered. "We need to get out. We need to get out, now."

But just as they made to quit the camp, a skinny scavenger in desert gear and goggles stood before him. A scout. He had been sent to assess the situation, and now, seeing only two, he decided to take his chances and prevent father and son from leaving with his water. A sudden rush of adrenalin shot through Jake as he stared at the machete in the scout's hands and thought about what that blade could do to him or his son.

Kai stepped nervously behind his father.

He watched the scavenger take menacing steps toward them. But Jake didn't seem worried. He seemed calm and focused with his hands slowly feeling for something at his side. Having found what he was looking for, quick as a flash, Jake let loose a savage cry and attacked the scavenger with his metal pipe.

But the scavenger anticipated the attack and dodged the pipe by a hair. He then lunged with his own attack, and Jake parried and moved out of the way while Kai tensed and held the handle of his knife, hoping he wouldn't have to use it. But knowing that he would to protect his father.

The scavenger came again. Again, Jake dodged a savage deathblow. The scavenger cursed him, raised the machete high above his head, and charged. Flashes of moonlight reflected off the dull blade. Jake quickly maneuvered out of the way at the last possible second and let his pipe smash against the scavenger's back.

Instantly the scavenger lost his footing and slipped in the dust and rocks and saw his life flash before his eyes as though his soul knew something his mind wouldn't accept. As though his soul knew this was the end. It wasn't a life story flashing in

QWAVA

reverse before his eyes as the scavenger remembered from the old movies from the old world. It was
something else. Moments. Moments that had been
meaningful to his soul. Being pulled out of a great
darkness to see his mother's eyes for the first time.
Swimming in a lake with his father. The first time he
had seen his wife at an amusement park. Holding his
newborn daughter and saying her name for the first
time. Kira. And then, the flashes stopped. Stopped
as though his mind knew the rest would only amplify
the horror of facing the unknown and unknowable.
The wars and rebellions. Killing others for water. All
of it he forget. His mind focused on one thing and
one thing only--to lift his soul above the darkness
with the beautiful and wonderful, with the sublime.
And there on the ground, he smiled with the image
of his newborn daughter in his arms and a strange
euphoric feeling suddenly and unexpectedly rushed
through every cell of his being like something divine.
Jake didn't hesitate.

It was a matter of life and death. And so,
before the scavenger had a chance to regain himself, as he clambered on the ground with a strange

QWAVA

smile on his face, Jake plunged on top of him with a terrible blow to the shoulders. The scavenger gasped as a momentary wave of blackness filled his vision but not the memory-the one memory he held on to like the last drop of water in the world.
The second blow went to the scavenger's hands as they instinctively came up to protect his face.
Instantly the forearms cracked into bits and pieces under the force of the rusty metal pipe. Splotches of black, and bright stars obstructed his vision as each blow sent doses of endorphins to ease the suffering and prepare him for his departure. When the scavenger couldn't feel or hold his broken arms up anymore to protect his face--

It was over.

His face and head caved in under a rapid fire succession of blows that shocked Kai as blood splattered this way and that; but the scene didn't scare him as this wasn't the first time he had seen his father kill a scavenger.

The scavenger stared up at Jake without seeing him as the dark blood filled his eyes and the world went dark. But even then Jake did not stop.

QWAVA

Blow after blow Jake pulverized the head until it was just a wet spot in the dust. Exhausted, he pulled himself away, grabbed Kai by the shoulder, and rushed into the darkness before the others found their friend, or what they would assume to be their friend. Jake knew these scavengers would take the rest of the water they had unwillingly left at the camp, and then they would proceed to track them across the Pacific. There was nothing else left in the world to hunt but each other. Maybe they were the last few people left in the world. Maybe they were the last. He wasn't sure. What he knew was that he hadn't seen another bird or rodent for a long time. Maybe weeks. And what he also knew was that there were fewer and fewer camps, and the camps they did happen upon were scenes of death and desperation with increasing incidences of cannibalism.
Jake and Kai traveled throughout the cool night and sought shelter in an old sunken wreck from the old world just before dawn. All day Jake watched the dusty horizon with his binoculars as Kai sat beside him wanting to ask him questions about the old world, but not wanting to disturb him when he knew

they were in being hunted like simple animals. He could see his father was deep in thought, thinking about ways to lose the scavengers, thinking about where to go next, thinking about the man he had killed, and muttering a silent prayer now and then, asking for forgiveness. Not from the universe. Not from God. From the man, explaining to him that he had left him with no other choice and that under other circumstances they might have been great friends. His father had killed many men, and women, and every time there was deep reverence for the life he had taken. It wasn't personal. It was never personal. It was always survival.

When night came again, they were on foot, pushing toward an unknown destination, hoping to Eden, or hoping to find another camp with water and food. By the end of the day as the white shimmering sun began to sink in the sky, they didn't find a camp or water or food. What they did find was cool shade under the skeletal remains of a blue whale. Kai stared at the great white bones in wonder. Seeing the curiosity in his son's eyes, Jake explained: "A blue whale. They were massive, and they swam free

QWAVA

in the oceans until the oceans disappeared." Jake unwittingly sighed as he remembered the past, and then he pulled himself out of his despair to recount everything he remembered about these majestic creatures.

"Were they dangerous?" Kai asked when his father finished his ode to blue whales.

"No. Not to people. Maybe to other fish. But not to people."

"Wish I could have seen one…not like this…" He indicated the massive bones arching overhead.

"Wish you could have seen one, too. They were something else."

Once again Kai could see his father drift away on a memory, thinking about the old times and the old world when water and life were abundant and everywhere and, sadly, taken for granted. "Were there others like it?" Kai asked after a silence.

"Other kinds? Other whales, you mean?"

Kai nodded. That's what he meant.

Jake smiled affectionately. "Sure. Dozens, even hundreds." His voice went low and melancholy.

QWAVA

"The oceans were big blue galaxies. Each one had a billion billion species, some big as whale, other small like snails, even smaller. And every year we'd discover new life in this great blue galaxy. It was like the oceans actually created life. It was like the water was magic…like it was alive and conscious and always wanting to create…like water was the soul of the world…"

Jake fell silent and thought about his words, about the possibility that water was not just an element that supported life, but was in fact life itself. Life sustaining life. Life rejuvenating life. Life creating life in a way far beyond human comprehension. It was a strange thought, and he shook it from his mind, and continued about the old world:

"Used to swim every day with your grandfather in the ocean, and he was really upset that we were bottling water and selling it because he just couldn't understand it; he couldn't understand how the corporations had made it so they could own water. He used to think that was as absurd as trying to own air until they did that too. I can't imagine what he would have said to all this now. He probably would have said that bottling and trying to own water was the first sign of what they were planning for us. That's what he would have said and he would have probably been right. I thank god he didn't have to see this." He gestured and indicated the desert surrounding him. "But he would have sensed it coming. Your grandfather had a strong instinct like you. I see a lot of him in you." He turned to Kai. "I wish things had been different. I wish you had known a different world."

"I remember swimming," Kai put in. He loved his talks with his father. They helped him forget, and they made him feel closer to his father; not as a son, but as a friend.

"You do? How could you? You were so young."

Kai shrugged his shoulders. He couldn't explain it, but he remembered. He had flashes of lying on a surfboard watching the horizon with his father who dove in and out of the water playing peekaboo with him. Sometimes he was with his father and mother and he was a little older. Maybe three. It was just him on the board with his parents

QWAVA

pulling the board here and there in the calm morning water. He remembered the blueness of it all; blue everywhere, the sky and the sea merging at the horizon into one beautiful thing; and now there was only the greyness of it all; the rock, sand and dunes wherever the eye looked. It was hard to believe he was still in the same world.

Still Kai dreamed of these moments. He dreamed of others as well, but those moments he wasn't sure if they were actual memories or stories his father and mother put in him.

He other strange dreams, dreams that couldn't possibly have been memories, dreams of his grandfather teaching his father how to surf as a child. It was strange. Strange because his father was so young then, almost his age, and Kai hadn't even been born yet; and yet, it was like he was right there, watching and observing his father and grandfather swimming and surfing in the breathing ocean. The feeling was not unlike that of being the cool ocean wind guiding and protecting the man his soul would one day choose to be mentor, guide, and protector-his father.

QWAVA

Choosing his parents-that's what his mother believed.

His mother had believed and on many occasions had told him that the soul has to make some important choices before it takes the plunge from the spiritual to the material. According to his mother, he had chosen her. For what reason she didn't know. For what reason she couldn't explain. But she had believed he had chosen her even before she had met his father. In fact she went so far as to say that he had helped them meet. She went on to explain that souls not only choose their parents, but sometimes they actually play the part of cupid as they silently and secretly create a sequence of events that help the chosen ones bump into one another. It was a strange theory. And his mother had believed in all kinds of strange mystical things that Kai didn't necessarily believe in.

When once he had told his mother that he kept on dreaming of being rescued by a massive black and white fish in the middle of the ocean, she grew very silent; then she explained to him that it wasn't a fish, that it was an orca, a killer whale, and that she didn't know if he had been saved by one or not, but that once when he was a toddler he had once been pulled out by an undercurrent and that it was a miracle when they found him floating far out in ocean. Not only floating but talking and laughing, as though there had been nothing to fear. No one knew who or what he had been babbling and laughing with, but not far away someone had spotted not one but several orcas.

Kai then told her that in his dream the orcas had kept him afloat and that they could speak to him with their thoughts, warning him about what would happen to the world. That's when she made him promise not to tell his father about the dream, saying he didn't believe in these new age spiritual things but that she wanted to know more, explaining that the orca was his totem animal, his guardian. Kai had no idea what she had meant by this, and then she explained that whenever his subconscious needed to guide or protect him, it would do so in the form of an orca or orcas, and they would come to him in his dreams and they would help him understand whatever he needed to understand.

QWAVA

As far as he could remember Kai had always had dreams of orcas and as far as he knew he had never seen one in real life. As far as he knew. Maybe a pack of orcas had saved him when he was a toddler, or maybe not. Whether he had been saved by orcas or not, he could never know and would never know because his father didn't even want to hear this idea of a totem animal that came to you in your dreams to help you. But the dream felt real, too real, and many times he doubted it was a dream at all. Sometimes it felt more like a memory, an old memory resurfacing from his past.

There was a long silence as Jake scanned the horizon for scavengers, gazing now and then at the sky, praying for a drizzle, or even a rain. After some time he sighed and said: "We sure didn't realize what we had...." He shook his head trying to understand what had happened and how they could be so careless with what he knew to be the most valuable resource in the universe. He sighed deeply and went inward for a moment. He shook his head and Kai could see he was thinking and having a deep and profound conversation with himself. His

QWAVA

lips moved slightly and he answered his own whispered questions with mingled shame and frustration. At last he said aloud: "And we thought they were here to help us." He laughed to himself, laughed at the absurdity of trusting the Ancients. "To bring peace and enlightenment…to bring us to a higher state of spiritual evolution…how foolish were we…how foolish…."

Jake laughed to himself again; historically some of the most evil events and people came camouflaged or even hidden behind a thick, disarming veil of peace and spirituality. India before the great and endless protests of the 'untouchables' was an example. For years the country had hidden behind Gandhi and yoga, but when the revolts broke out no one even suspected there was such a thing as a low caste slave, that they were not only physical slaves but spiritual slaves, and that they made up more than a third of the country's population. Beyond the veil people soon discovered that India was the exact opposite of what it propagated itself to be in the world. He even remembered how surprised he had been to discover that the country that was perceived as the most peaceful and spiritual was in fact the most violent and oppressive to its low caste slaves. Far more violent and oppressive than South Africa under Apartheid, and yet because of the veil they were exempt from the international sanctions that had helped crush Apartheid and freed an entire people.

India was the only country in the world that could hold on to its slave system of Caste Apartheid for as long as it had because of the veil, because all corporations benefited from a cheap middle class made possible by a slave class, and because no one could see past Gandhi or yoga, even though Gandhi, himself had compared the caste system to Jim Crow or Apartheid, and had tried to end Caste Apartheid when India had been freed by the British, but had been shamelessly and brutally assassinated by a high caste terrorist trying to protect the high caste right to rule over minorities and untouchables as living gods. It had even shocked him to discover that these high castes had little or no regard for people born out of India. They were called lechers, and lechers were lower than untouchables, and in their

QWAVA

caste hierarchy lechers were below the lowest of the low. Lower even than animals born in India. It was a shock to him and his family to discover that there still existed a place in the world with slaves, and when the mainstream media began to propagated this idea that the Ancients were here for peace and spiritually, Jake thought of India, thought of the veil that protected it from international scrutiny and economic sanctions, and a cold shuddering fear shook his bones to the marrow.

"I hate them," Kai said, joining the conversation. "I wish I could do to them what they did to us."

Jake shook his head. "No one deserves what they did to us. Not even them."

"I hate them."

"I hate what they did."

There was a long silence between father and son as Kai pondered the difference between 'I hate them' and 'I hate what they did'. There was a lesson in those words; one Jake didn't feel he needed to explain as he kept an eye out for scavengers. After some time Kai asked: "Will we be okay?" Jake turned to him without an answer, without knowing what to say or how to answer. "What will happen to us?" Kai whispered.

Jake could only shake his head. "Don't know," he said. "Don't know..."

"What if we can't find water?"

"We'll find water."

"What if there's nothing more to eat?"

"We'll find something."

"But I haven't seen anything-"

"We're just not in the right place," Jake answered in an attempt to keep his son from despairing. "There's Eden and it's not far from here, and there are lots of children and food and that's where we're heading. So I don't think we need to worry. It's just a matter of getting there."

"Is it true?" Kai was beginning to doubt this place called 'Eden' existed.

Jake hesitated, then he answered: "Yeah, it's true. Lots of water and kids and food. And enough for everyone so we don't need to fight any-more."

"Enough to wash?"

"Enough to wash."

"Enough to swim?"

Jake's head fell. "Stop asking so many questions. Save your energy."

Kai nodded, and leaned his head against his father's leg and closed his eyes. He didn't know how long he had fallen asleep but when his father shook him awake with a sudden urgency it was dark and ominous and in the moonlight he could see shadowy figures in the distance walking toward them.

Scavengers.

Silently, Kai rose, grabbed his flasks and quickly followed his father through pools of moonlight and shadow. They walked quietly and lightly and tried their best not to make tracks in the dust and dirt, and they walked endlessly until once again the orange and red dawn appeared on the horizon and they were standing before a small rocky mountain.

Jake pointed to a small opening above. A cave. "Climb up, and I'll join you after."

"Where will you go?"

"Going to lead them away, then I'll backtrack," he said. "I have a feeling they're tracking us in the day. If they are, they'll catch up to us."

An indescribable pain instantly shot through Kai. Without knowing why, Kai launched himself on his father and embraced. "I want to go," he said. "I want to go with you."

"Better if you stay." He pushed away and handed him his flasks. "Take a sip if you're thirsty but no more."

"Don't go." He didn't know why he was reacting like this, but something inside was tugging at his heart, telling him to stop his father from leaving, telling him that he may never see him again.

Jake sighed, understood his boy's fears and anxieties, and would have stayed, but leading the scavengers away from their temporary refuge was not an option. It was necessary to their survival. "It's just for a bit," he said and patted Kai's head. "I won't be gone too long. I swear it. But I need to do this. You do understand?"

Kai nodded that he understood. Just because he understood didn't mean he liked the idea of being separated from his father.

QWAVA

"Good," Jake said, glancing off toward the shimmering horizon. "They won't stop until they've found us-" His voice was low and faraway. He took a deep breath, and said a prayer. Then he made to go, and once again Kai suddenly and unexpectedly embraced him again, held him tight, and didn't want to let go, refused to let go.

"I'll see you soon," Jake hugged his son back, then reluctantly pushed away, noticing unshed tears in his son's eyes. He knew the boy had a strong intuition like his mother, which worried him because it was possible he sensed something, but he also knew that his intuition was sometimes wrong. Sometimes. He caressed his son's hair, gave him a long affectionate look, turned from the mountain and began walking away, pressing heavy and hard with every step he took as he lead the scavengers away from their temporary refuge.

Kai watched his father disappear in a cloud of dust and debris. When he was gone, he turned and grabbed his father's rucksack and flasks and began hiking up the side of the mountain. It wasn't long before he entered the gloom of the cave and

QWAVA

found rusted old equipment like an old moonshine distillery. He observed the equipment, and the mingled skeletal remains of humans and rats and other small rodents scattered over the rocky floor. A distillery.

Not a moonshine distillery. A water distillery. An improvised metal and plastic contraption that could extract and condense water from a corpse so as not to waste any moisture that might be caught in the muscle, bone, or cartilage.

Kai closed his eyes and tried not to think of the fate of all the cracked and charred skulls he could see scattered around him. When he opened his eyes, he kicked the contraption out of the way and sat in the coolness of the shadows and prayed for his father's safety.

Slowly, his heavy eyes began to close as prayer turned to dreams. Then he was a little boy again. A little boy on a surf board floating on a great blue expanse of water, watching the dawn with his parents. He saw them in his mind's eye, and he wished he could live in that moment forever. That was a good moment. Blue above. Blue below. Blue

QWAVA

all around; blue, and the sound of the soft, breathing ocean with the birds tumbling and circling and chattering in the sky above.

He could hear the birds, and he could even see them. Tumbling and twirling through the air, diving in and out of the clear, fresh water. His father had told him there had been thousands of species of every possible size and color. Red and green. Yellow and blue. Orange and yellow. Purple and yellow. Tiny ones. Small ones. Ones the size of a child. Others smaller than a finger. The whole planet had been an Eden. Green land enclosed by blue oceans with colorful birds swimming in the sky and colorful fish swimming in the ocean. He could hardly imagine or dream of such a place in the endless desert he found himself in. And they had lost it all.

How Kai wished he could travel back in time and warn the world about the future, about what they would lose and how they would lose it. But somehow he sensed even a time machine would be useless, and they would still lose everything.

It didn't matter what he said. No one would listen.

QWAVA

His father had told him that by the time the Ancients were ready for their harvest, the people were no longer interested by the truth and far more interested in a genre of entertainment called the news. Biased opinions, not perspectives. Sound bites, not stories. No backstories, no history, no research, no opposing views, just some pretty face spewing off a sound bite as truth undeniable that the masses would swallow unquestioningly so as to get on with their harried, microwave days where no one seemed to have time to do anything anymore but make money and pay taxes. The Ancients and those they controlled in the media and government had artificially made it so no one had time to think or form opinions anymore.

High taxes. High cost of living. No security. Just fear. Fear of sickness. Fear of death. Fear of poverty. Everyone working more hours in a day so they could barely make ends meet in a system created to institutionalize the world and turn living, breathing, thinking human beings with infinite potential into unquestioning cogs in a machine with little or no time to take care of their children, spend time with their parents, or ponder the sound bites that they were being asked to swallow. It was generic daycares and generic jobs and generic old folk's homes with everyone drinking the same generic drinks eating the same generic food and discussing the same generic sound bites from the same generic perspective they had consumed the night before from the same generic news broadcast.

It hadn't always been that way. It had gotten that way one small law at a time and had ended up that way and had done so about the same time when the corporations began to privatize and sell water.

Kai's grandfather was of another time. He had opinions, and he questioned things, especially the sound bites he was being asked to swallow, and he was the last of a dying generation. Everyone else, even his own father, was quite satisfied with the sound bite that was crafted not to expand and inform but to entertain and indoctrinate.

Kai couldn't explain everything he needed to explain in a sound bite. He needed time and the opportunity to show the world how the Ancients had

QWAVA

infiltrated humanity and how they slowly but surely helped humanity with new technology for one reason and one reason only: so humanity could help them prepare the atmosphere for a perfect harvest. His father had told him that there had been many attempts to expose what the Ancients were doing to the world. But no one listened. Not really. Not because they couldn't, but because they didn't care. Cogs didn't care. People cared, and that's precisely why the Ancients had first worked so very hard to reduce people to cogs in their machine.

There had been many attempts, and his father had kept a journal of those who had tried to speak out against the Ancients and had been vilified by the media. The media had ridiculed anyone who spoke against them, and they had severely down-played warnings against what was happening to the planet. The media, in essence, had painted the Ancients as interplanetary monks here on a peaceful mission to help humanity spiritually and technologi-cally. It had been called a techno-spiritual revolution. It had been anything but.

Kai gazed at the blue ocean surrounding

QWAVA

him. There in his dream he lay on his father's surfboard with his father pulling him deeper and deeper into the great blue. Then, all of sudden, his father stopped, turned to face him with troubled eyes, and told him to get up. "Get up," he said. "Kai, you need to wake up. Wake up now."

But Kai didn't want to get up. He wanted to stay in his cool blue dream for as long as he possibly could.

"Listen to me," his father said firmly, "Something has happened, but you're going to be okay. Do you understand? You are going to be okay so long as you listen to me."

"I don't understand," Kai said. "I don't..."

"They will find you, they need to find you. You will help them, and they will help you. You will help many others before it's too late. But first you must get up. You must get up now. You must find me. You must find me, so they can find you. Get up, kiddo, get up...get up now!"

Suddenly a noise startled Kai awake. Crumbling rocks and the sound of someone clambering up the mountain.

QWAVA

It took him a moment to adjust his mind to the dusty cool night. He rose slowly and looked around for his father, but his father was nowhere to be found. He told himself he would tell him about his dream and he focused on trying to remember it, but the more he tried to remember it the more he forgot. His father had told him something in his dream and it was like he was really there, really him, and it had been important. Then he heard it again. The crunch of stone and the crumbling of rocks.

"Dad," he whispered. "Dad..." He stared out into the darkness and took small careful steps toward the mouth of the cave. He peered outside. There, climbing and clambering up toward him he could see a dark silhouette. "Dad..." His voice trailed off in uncertainty.

Whoever was climbing would not answer or could not answer him. The silhouette stopped suddenly, seemed to peer up at Kai, then continued up toward him without saying a word. Then it dawned on him that his father wasn't saying anything just in case there were scavengers in the area. So Kai slowly made his way down to meet his father, the

QWAVA

whole while trying to remember his dream, trying to remember what his father had told him, but he couldn't remember any of it.

Inching closer and closer toward the dark silhouette, Kai scrutinized the silhouette. "Dad," he whispered. "Dad…" Suddenly a flash of moonlight reflecting off a blade illuminated the face. With a terrible gasp, Kai realized he was walking toward a scavenger. But by the time he realized the man wasn't his father, and that he was young and oriental, it was too late. With a wild scream, the scavenger charged Kai, grabbed him and thrust him down against the hard trail.

The scavenger cursed the boy as he took menacing steps toward him, promising he would have fun killing him. Gathering himself, Kai quickly scrambled to his feet, but the scavenger rushed in and sent him flying against the narrow trail with a powerful kick in the ribs. Kai rolled over the narrow ground and nearly fell off the edge and down the mountain to his death. The scavenger laughed again, and trying to keep his balance, moved toward Kai as Kai rose

QWAVA

once again to his feet and made for his knife. But just as he pulled it out the scavenger snatched his wrist and squeezed; he squeezed and crushed the wrist until Kai screamed in utter agony and released the knife one crumpled finger at a time. The knife fell forty feet to the rocky ground and the scavenger once again thrust Kai to the ground. This time Kai rolled off the side but a lucky hand grabbed hold of a crag.

With difficulty, Kai pulled himself up onto the trail and the scavenger laughed aloud and seemed to be amusing himself with this boy. Then every time Kai tried to stand the scavenger he kicked him back to the ground. Kai prayed inwardly for his father, prayed for help, but his father never came. It was then, when he realized he was on his own. Suddenly he remembered a few wrestling techniques and tricks his father had taught him.

Instantly his hand reached out and grabbed a fistful of dirt and began to crawl away from his attacker. When the scavenger went to kick and humiliate him yet another time, Kai turned suddenly and thrust the dirt in his eyes. Thousands of dirt and

QWAVA

dust particles filled the scavenger's dry white eyes and he screamed in mingled anger and pain, giving Kai enough time to scramble to his feet and run up the mountain.

He didn't run too far. He didn't need to. He wasn't running away. He just need some distance to execute a sweeping tackle his father had taught him. Taking distance, he turned to face the scavenger who continued to curse in Japanese as he desperately tried to rub the dirt out of his eyes.
The scavenger expected Kai to try to bolt, to run up the mountain. But Kai didn't run. There was no use. There was nowhere to go. It was a dead end up there in the cave, and he thought that maybe he could best this scavenger. True, he couldn't do much against an adult, especially without a weapon, but he could tackle him, nail him in the legs and knock him over like a bowling pin.

So Kai lowered his gaze, focused, then, to the scavenger's surprise, ran as fast as he could down the trail as the scavenger laughed and extended his arms to greet the boy. But just as he neared the scavenger, Kai suddenly dropped, hit the ground

QWAVA

at an angle, and slid feet first into the armored shins like a bowling ball.

Instantly the scavenger dropped face first to the ground and rolled over the side of the trail, desperately grabbing hold of the ledge at the last moment.

Without thinking, Kai went for the kill. It was him or the scavenger. There was nothing else. He grabbed a boulder and stared at the hands and didn't let it drop right away. This was it. If he smashed this man's hands, he would fall to his death. If he smashed this man's hands he would kill a man. There was no doubt about it. The scavenger looked up at the boy looming over him with the boulder and waited. When he saw Kai hesitate, he began to beg for his life.

But Kai couldn't trust him. His father had once let a man go, and that man had killed his mother. There was no compassion, no mercy in this world. Not anymore. Maybe, he thought, there had never been. Just a semblance of empathy and civility hiding the truth of their existence. And the truth was simply this. Life lived off of other life. But maybe this wasn't the whole truth. Maybe this was only a part truth and the conditions of the world made it seem like it was the only truth.

Suddenly Kai felt a surge of adrenalin rush through him. He stared below, but didn't see the desperate, helpless, begging scavenger. All he saw was red, and all he felt was the will to live and the need to see his father again. And so, with a terrible cry, he pounded and pummeled those hands until they fractured and could not hold on to anything anymore. Instantly the scavenger saw moments flash before his eyes as though his soul sensed the end. Moments that ate away the fear and filled him with good thoughts. Seeing his mother for the first time. Being thrown in the air by his father. Learning how to wield a katana from his grandfather. Meeting his girlfriend for the first time in a restaurant. And her smile. He held on to the image and didn't think of the rest. Didn't think of the wars. Didn't think of the rebellions. The thirst and hunger. Just her. Her in that moment, and that moment wasn't like eternity, it was eternity. A moment later the scavenger fell to his death, crushing his skull and dashing his brains against the

QWAVA

hard rocky bottom. With a strange euphoric feeling the scavenger stared above at the silhouette of the boy above as the darkness slowly filled his eyes and the world went dark.

Staring at the crushed and contorted corpse below, Kai gasped, then stumbled back on his haunches. He had killed a man. The first ever. For a long while he stared at the moon-lit sky and tried to forget what he had done and prayed for his father to return soon.

When dawn finally returned, revealing a wasteland of dust, rock and dirt, Kai sat up and scrambled to his feet, searching all around, searching for his father. But his father was still nowhere in sight. "Dad!" he called out. "Dad!" He looked down below. "Dad!" He waited for an answer; when none came something terrible pulled inside him. He had never been separated from his father this long before. Something inside told him to inspect the body. He inched toward the edge and looked down. The splattered corpse, and there next to the body his father's rucksack.

"No!" he cried in despair. "No..."

QWAVA

And he dashed down the trail toward the body, falling
now and then in his panic, then scrambling and
vaulting back up with impossible speed and strength.
When he reached the bottom, he ignored the broken
body and grabbed hold of the rucksack. Instantly he
pulled it away from the blood and gore. Then he
loomed over the body and gnashed his teeth with
rage.

"What did you do!"

He heaved.

"Where is he you son-of-a-bitch!"

He waited for a response he knew would
never come. Desperate, helpless, alone, he continued nonetheless. "Where is he?" He cursed and
yelled at the corpse-yelled again and again, and he
only stopped when he felt he was about to collapse
with rage and exhaustion. Then he took a moment to
gather himself, and he asked himself what his father
would do in his situation; then, answering himself, he
looted the corpse and found a flask of water, almost
empty, and in another pocket he found two shining
tin cans of undetermined food contents.

Without a second to lose, Kai took the

QWAVA

water and food, grabbed the rucksack, threw it around his shoulder and headed into the white shimmering day, tracking the scavenger's footprints in the dirt, searching for his father, praying with all his heart and soul that he was still alive.

Kai searched all day for his father, calling out for him every minute as he followed a trail or lost a trail or found another trail. It was only toward dusk when he picked up another trail of three scavengers which he thought might lead to his father. Carefully and stealthily he tracked the scavengers through wrecks and caverns to a small oasis of water near a collection of giant whale bones. Losing hope, he searched the area in the growing darkness, but found nothing. But then, just as he was about to turn away and sniff out another trail, he spotted something beyond a rock formation, and then he thought he heard something, too. He narrowed his gaze. Bodies. Three. Lying on the ground. With his heart in his mouth, Kai instantly rushed toward the scene. He stopped at the first body. A Japanese woman. The scavenger's skull had been crack by something metal and heavy.

QWAVA

Probably his father's metal pipe. Quite possibly the mother of the young man he had sent plummeting to his death. Then, suddenly, he heard it again. A man whispering a name. Not his name. Another name. Toshi.

Kai turned toward the dying man. As he inched closer to him, he noticed he was an older Japanese man with grey hair and a deeply scarred face. He was still breathing, barely, through a cracked nose and a mouthful of blood and broken teeth. He looked up at Kai. Then he gazed beyond his shoulders for Toshi. When he didn't see him, his eyes grew grave and faraway. The man peered up at Kai and Kai peered back down at him for a long while. They said nothing. Just stared, and for some reason they didn't feel like enemies, and yet instinctively Kai knew that they were.

With a deep breath Kai turned toward the other body and prayed to find another member of this man's clan. But he immediately noticed that the body was of a different size and build, and then there was his intuition, this thing pulling in him, telling him it was his father, slowing him down with every

QWAVA

step he took until he was barely making progress.
He took slow, uneasy steps toward the body.
When at last he reached the corpse, he stopped and
stared at the back of the head in the darkness. He
just stared at it as though he didn't want to know.
After some time he kneeled before the man and
turned him over and instantly froze at the sight. He
wanted to say something, but nothing came out as
he stared into his father's lifeless eyes. "No…" His
voice trailed off in tears as he pulled a short katana
blade out of his father's stomach and held him close.
"Please, no…please, Dad…no….don't do this…I
need you…please…please…."

      Kai held him for almost the entire night. He
never felt so alone in his life. More than alone. He
felt like the last man on Earth. Then a sudden gurgle
reminded him that he wasn't alone. His father's killer
was still alive, lying not ten feet from him. The rage
blood filled his mind and heart and he turned toward
the dying man who was still mumbling the name.
Toshi. Toshi…

      Slowly, almost like he was in a nightmare,
he grabbed the blood-stained blade that had killed

QWAVA

his father from the ground and stood fierce and erect. Drenched head-to-toe in his father's blood, he peered at the man and did not move. Then, one small, exhausted step at a time he marched toward him with the blade throwing spears of reflected moonlight in his face or on the ground beside him. When Kai reached the dying man, he halted and listened to the name and watch the man squirm with the hope he would see his son again. The dying man looked up a Kai. "You killed him," he said with blood and teeth fragments sputtering out of his mouth. "My son..."

Kai nodded. He had killed his son. His son had been his first kill, and now he would be second. Tears filled the dying man's eyes and they began to stream down his face to mix with the coagulated blood on his cheek and neck. He closed his eyes and said his son's name over and over again. Then he opened them, and there wasn't anger or hate in his eyes for the boy who had killed his son, only a strange understanding and a request. "Please," the man gurgled. "Please..."

Somehow Kai instinctually understood what

the man had meant. He nodded, feeling his hate and anger strangely leaving him. Then he kneeled beside the man. With endless tears flowing down his face, the man reached out to Kai and held the hand that held the hilt of the katana. "I'm sorry," he said, and Kai could see he was sincere, truly sincere, and that he wished life hadn't forced him in a situation where he had to do the things he had had to do to keep his family alive.

Kai said nothing. But new tears began. He would never talk to his father again, never hear his stories, never hear his laugh or see himself reflected in his eyes. After a silence, the man pulled the katana closer to his chest, placing the blade over his heart. "Please..."

Without a word, without anger, Kai watched the blade as it flashed spears of white light moonlight in his eyes. The man remembered holding a new-born boy and held that moment in his heart like eternity. Then Kai closed his eyes and pushed the blade deep into the man's heart. The man didn't scream out in pain. He merely sighed and released his life's breath, staring up at Kai as the warm darkness filled

QWAVA

his eyes and the world went dark and he was once again with his family.

After a moment, Kai stood on shaky legs, and returned to his father. He held him close and cried, not knowing what he would do next, or what would happen next, only knowing that he felt alone, really alone, alone like the last man on Earth, and this time he was.

It was the hot shimmering afternoon of the next day when he saw the space cruiser the size of a shopping mall in the sky. He finally released his father and gazed up at it and felt indescribable and incalculable hate for the Ancients, wishing with all his heart to one day do to their planet what they had done to his. Then, staring up at the sky, he saw a small spherical vessel suddenly dash out of the cruiser and it seemed to make its way toward him. As the vessel headed toward him, he rushed toward the man he had killed, pulled out the katana that had killed his father and hid the weapon behind his back and waited.

For some reason or another Kai figured the Ancients had returned for the last of the water and

QWAVA

had spotted him and perhaps wanted to make him a
slave on their planet as he had heard they had done
with some rebels. This Ancient would be his third kill.
The hum of the vessel grew louder and louder until it
flashed in the sunlight and hovered just above him;
within seconds there was a soft hiss as it began to
descend before him. When it had landed, there was
yet another soft hiss as the shiny metallic door slid
open and an Ancient stepped out.

"My name is Azan," the Ancient said, sensing the
boy's fear, taking a small cautious step toward him.
He wore a black metallic space suit with biolumines-
cent blue sensors monitoring his vitals. His hair was
as white as his skin and his skin was as white as
snow. "I have come to help you. I am a medical doc-
tor specializing in humanoids and exoskelatoids."
Kai stared into the blue eyes of his enemy. "You
destroyed us and left us with nothing." He laughed at
the absurdity of an Ancient wanting to help him. It
didn't make any sense. To the Ancients humans
were bugs. Lower than bugs, at least bugs on their
planet. "Now you say you want to help me." He

began to move round Azan, scrutinizing him, preparing to pounce.

"I understand how you feel, but I am not like the others. I am here to help."

"That's what they said. That's what they all said."

Kai emphasized the 'they'.

Azan nodded. He understood. He didn't expect Kai to trust him after his kind had turned his rich blue planet into a sweltering heap of dust and dirt. "You will to have to trust me. There is no chance for survival here. There is nothing to live off of. There is nothing to sustain you. Not for very long. The planet is dead. Nothing survives on a dead planet."

Kai continued to circle him. "I'll take my chances--" And with those words he suddenly withdrew the katana and sailed toward Azan. He didn't see the Ancient react. Didn't even notice him flinch. All he saw was a blur. And all he knew was that within a moment he was on the ground with the Ancient looming above him, holding the katana in his white hand and appraising it.

Kai didn't remember Ancients being fast or

QWAVA

strong. Usually, they were weak and slow and reliant on their superior technology or other beings to do their fighting. Not this one. Clearly, not this one.

Gathering himself, Kai stood with difficulty as Azan stepped toward him and handed back the katana, saying: "No chance. There is no chance. And I am afraid you are the last of your kind."
Kai shook his head, refusing to believe this, remembering all the talks and vivid descriptions of Eden. His father said there were hundreds, even thousands, parents and children. Azan could see that Kai doubted his words. "I'm afraid you are." Azan confirmed. "The planet is dead."

"It's not. We'll start over again."

Azan cocked his head curiously. "Who is we?"

"There are others, up North..." Kai turned toward the North and stared for a long while.

Azan took a step closer to Kai and felt very sorry for him. After a silence he said in a low voice: "No. There is no life up North. There is no water to return life. And what is left, is not enough The planet is dead."

QWAVA

Kai shook his head and refused to believe what he was hearing. "There's a place...a place with parents and children, and water...plenty of water for all of us...so much water that we don't need to fight or hurt each for it..."

Azan shook his head gravely. "I am afraid not. We have searched and scanned the entire planet. I can assure you, there is no more water, and you are the last of your kind. The planet is dead, and you will be too if you do not come with me." Azan paused, and waited for the boy to respond. When Kai said nothing, he continued: "I know it is hard to trust me because of others like me did to you. But you must believe I am here to help you."

Kai turned to regard him, then he turned back toward the North. He didn't say anything. He just stared. There was nothing left. He turned to his father's body, and stumbled backward and fell to his haunches as the realization flooded over him. There was no such place as Eden. There was nothing in the North. No parents, no children, no water, nothing. It was just a cliché his father had borrowed from cheap post-apocalyptic movies; a story he had

QWAVA

embellished to keep his hope alive. And it had worked. The Ancient peered down sadly at Kai. At last the Ancient said: "Stay here, and you will die. Come with me, and you will live."

Again, Kai didn't answer him. With the last of his strength, he dragged himself toward his father and took his hand. He already missed him; missed him in a way words could not describe; then, sudden tears appeared when he realized that he would never hear his stories again. He would never hear about his grandfather and the lakes, rivers and oceans and all the colorful and majestic creatures that lived in the great blue galaxies. He would never hear about the waves and how his grandfather had been some kind of surfing champion in the old times. They would never talk again. They would never talk about the family or the old days. It was just like when his mother had died. He had sensed their special talks would never happen again. He had sensed that all the talks about dreams and totem animals and spirituality his father liked to make fun of were over. And they were. And sometimes he felt into great panics when his being unconsciously wanted to talk to her but the oppressive finality of death rendered this impossible. At those times his father would calm him down and sing to him to help him fall asleep. Sometimes he would close his eyes, and thinking he was asleep he could hear his father whispering directly to him, telling him things about the past he didn't really talk about, telling him about how he used to dance with him every morning and night when he was a baby and how only Louis Armstrong would help him fall asleep, telling him all these things that these events that he had done, telling him how he was his greatest joy, the best thing in his life, and that every day was a divine privilege to raise and take care of him-telling him how much he loved him. Telling him things that he didn't necessarily say while Kai was awake. When he was awake, it was the stories of the old world and facts and techniques on survival. It was all mind. When Kai shut his eyes and feigned sleep, it was all heart. And he loved to hear his father speak from the heart, and so he always feigned sleep before he actually fell asleep just to hear his father's words.

As Kai stared at his father wishing for more

QWAVA

time to talk about the old days, wishing to hear his
heart speak to him one more time, Azan stepped up
behind him and watched him. After a long moment,
Azan broke the silence, saying: "There are many
others like you on board."

"I don't want to go on board."

"You don't want to die either."

Kai thought about this and wasn't sure if he
wanted to die or not; everyone he had ever loved
was gone; even though it had never been, Eden was
gone; then he wondered who these others were and
he questioned: "There are many like me. From
Earth?"

"No."

"From other planets?"

Azan nodded. "Refugees."

"Refugees?"

"The last of many civilizations."

Kai pondered this, and he wondered how
many planets the Ancients had destroyed for life-giv-
ing qwava. At last he asked: "Where will we go?
What will I do?"

"You will survive."

QWAVA

Kai shook his head. Surviving-just surviving-was not enough. He would rather die the last of his kind on a desert planet than merely survive. "That's not enough. It's…not enough…I'd rather die here on my planet, than old up there, surviving."

Azan thought about this for a moment. Then he answered: "We will travel far. To places unimagined. To universes and planets you have never seen or ever thought possible before. We shall watch over these places. And we shall try to prevent such things from happening to other planets."

Kai turned to regard the Azan. "You mean you stopped them before."

"Sometimes we are not too late."

Kai turned back to his father.

"Come," Azan said, "We should go." Azan began toward the vessel, but Kai didn't budge.
"I'm not leaving him here like this," Kai said, and he grabbed his katana and began to carve and break the earth.

Azan stopped, turned and regarded the boy. At last he nodded and said: "I understand." Then he moved toward the skiff and returned with two metal

QWAVA

panels. He handed one to Kai, then he kneeled beside the boy and began to help him dig a hole to bury his father.

Kai stopped for a moment. Through his tears he watched the Ancient dig with him. It was the first time he had ever seen any Ancient do any labor let alone get on his knees and dig beside a lekka. He didn't know much about the Ancient religion, but he knew that they had a caste system that rendered the majority of the population slaves much like the Mayans. He had heard that on their planet they had slaves, slaves native to the planet, and slaves from other planets, and all of these slaves that were beneath them on the caste hierarchy were properly and systemically categorized into specific labors that could be identified by their last names, outfits and residences.

The Ancients were at the top of their cosmic caste system. They were the gods of the universe, and only they were allowed to read and interpret the spiritual texts of the Vak.

Kai also knew that according to the Ancient caste system beings born on other planets were the lowest of the low in the hierarchy. Lower even than animals and plant life born on their planet which they considered the most divine planet in all of creation. This is why they were usually able to destroy and plunder other planets without remorse or second thoughts.

It was their divine right.

Their godly right.

They were doing it to lekkas, and lekkas were the lowest of the low in the universe, and to the gods of the universe, who had been lucky enough to first have been born on the divine planet, and second to have been born an Ancient at the top of the caste system; killing a lekka was like killing a bug. In actuality killing a bug born on the divine planet was considered a graver crime than killing an evolved humanoid or exoskelatoid on another planet. One bug born on the divine planet was worth a million lekkas. This according to the laws of the Ancients.

It took hours to dig a hole big enough and deep enough to bury his father. When it was ready Kai said his final good-bye, kissed his father on the fore-

QWAVA

head, and took from his pocket his lucky dancing Hawaiian dancer that he used to mediate on before he fell asleep; a trick he used to help him remember the old world. Kai figured he could use it, too, for the same reasons; to help him remember the old world; to help him remember the old planet.
Kai pocketed the plastic Hawaiian girl, then turned to Azan and nodded. He was ready to bury his father. A moment later they hoisted him and lowered him gently into his grave. Through endless, silent tears Kai stared at him a long time until he was ready to say his final good-bye.

But he never really was, and so Azan began to slowly shovel the dry earth over his father for him. Kai stared at his father's eyes until they disappeared under a layer of dry earth, then Kai joined in with tears streaming down his face and off his chin, feeling alone, feeling more alone than he had ever been in his life, and feeling angry and helpless, wishing he could turn back time and hug him for just a little bit longer. He had lost more than a father. He had lost his mentor, protector, defender, his friend, and his very last link to his past, to his ancestors,

QWAVA

who his father had always kept alive with his endless stories of the past.

When the grave was covered, Kai closed his eyes and said a prayer for his father's soul. His mother had told him that the soul never moved too far away from a loved one if the loved one wished it to be so; and if the loved one wished it, wished it with all his heart, he could ask for that soul to accompany him on his life's journey. His father didn't believe in these things; he had even told her not to tell Kai these things, or give him strange ideas that might or might not be true. But it was her way of giving her boy hope, and, besides it wasn't for him to believe or edit or silence; he had his practical and historical stories while she had her stories of souls and guides and dreams and totem animals. In this way Kai had had a strong practical and spiritual upbringing, and between the both found the balance. And so just in case his mother was right, Kai closed his eyes and with all his soul he did as he had done when he had buried his mother. He thanked his father for getting him this far, he thanked him for always watching over him and protecting him, and

QWAVA

then…he thanked him for the stories and for always keeping his hope alive with his stories of Eden. At last he made the wish; but his wish was bigger than he had expected, much bigger, and what he wished for was much more than just his father and mother to accompany him on his life's journey, but all of his ancestors who had been responsible for bringing him to this point in his life where he was about to face a greater and bigger tyrant than any of them had ever faced.

Inwardly Kai asked that all his ancestors who were the whole reason for his existence to follow him and help him on this journey; he wished that they should come to him in his dreams to guide and protect him so that he could prevent the Ancients from doing to other planets what they had done to his. He didn't know if such a wish would work; but it didn't hurt to try. He had nothing to lose and everything to gain.

With his final wish, his eyes sprang open and he took his katana, took his rucksack with the computer and all the relics he had collected over the years, and he followed the dusty Ancient named

QWAVA

Azan into the skiff without knowing where he would end up or what he would do or who he would meet on board the massive generation ship hovering in the sky. Outlaws. Rebels. Refugees of destroyed planets. Somehow Kai sensed he would fit in. Somehow he sensed they would be to him a new family, and together they would help other civilizations remember and protect the divine resource, the most sacred resource in the universe--qwava--life-giving qwava.

www.ingramcontent.com/pod-product-compliance
Lightning Source LLC
Chambersburg PA
CBHW061042050726
47592CB00004B/1555

9 781927 028148